AR: no test available

W9-DBK-767

KIDNAPPED ON ASTARR

KIDNAPPED ON ASTARR

By Joan Lowery Nixon

Illustrated by Paul Frame

GARRARD PUBLISHING COMPANY
CHAMPAIGN, ILLINOIS

Library of Congress Cataloging in Publication Data

Nixon, Joan Lowery.
   Kidnapped on Astarr.

   SUMMARY: With a robot's help two children search for
a relative who has been kidnapped by the king on the
planet Astarr and accused of making secret war weapons.
   [1. Science fiction. 2. Kidnapping—Fiction]
I. Frame, Paul, 1913-   II. Title.
PZ7.N65Kh   [E]   80-11740
ISBN 0-8116-7450-9

CONTENTS

CHAPTER
1
The Search Begins

Kleep opened the door to her grandfather's laboratory and looked inside. Arko was bent over a reading table. Kleep went in, followed by Zibbit, her robot.

"Yeow!" Arko gasped with surprise as he looked up. He leaned back in his chair and took off the large pair of glasses that rested on his nose.

"Sorry," he said. "I was trying on these new superay glasses I invented. When you came in, all I could see were your bones."

Kleep reached for the glasses and tried them on.

Sometimes Arko let Kleep work with him in the laboratory. Kleep liked that. They'd worked together on Zibbit. Kleep was proud that Zibbit was programmed to have feelings. Not every robot on Astarr could mechanically laugh and cry.

But she hadn't worked with her grandfather on the new superay glasses. She thought they were exciting.

Now she looked through them at Zibbit. His metal gears and bolts were suddenly visible. Kleep could see a spot that needed some oiling. She giggled.

"They're wonderful, Grandfather," Kleep said. "May I borrow them for a while?" She took off the glasses and dropped them into her shirt pocket.

Before Arko could answer, the laboratory door burst op and Till raced into the room. "My mother has disappeared!" he cried to Arko.

"Someone must have forced her to leave. She wouldn't go away without leaving a message for me. All I found was this scrap of paper on the floor."

Till handed it to Arko. Kleep read the note over her grandfather's shoulder. Then she looked up at Till. "All the note says is 'Till—RU . . .,'" Kleep said. "What does 'RU' mean?"

Arko frowned while he thought. Kleep studied her grandfather. He was tall, and his hair was thick and curly and pink. "It's just like mine," Kleep thought.

She loved her grandfather. Sometimes he scolded her for rushing into things without thinking carefully. Sometimes he sighed and said she could be the noisiest person on Astarr. But his eyes twinkled when he looked at her. And he always had a warm hug when she needed it.

Arko's words cut into Kleep's thoughts. "'RU' could mean one of three things," he said. "One, the rare metal ruthenium. Falda and I are working with this in our new experiment."

"I know," Kleep said. "You want to invent something to anchor small craft at docks in outer space."

Arko nodded. "Two, our home planet, Ruel. And three, the people of Ruzena."

"But the people of Ruzena have had nothing to do with the rest of us on Astarr," Kleep said. "Ever since we came to live on their planet they have been unfriendly."

Till ran his hands through his dark hair. "We've got to find my mother!" he said.

Arko reached for the contactor and pressed a series of buttons. He spoke quickly. Then he put down the contactor and turned to Till.

"Falda has not taken a space flight to Ruel," he said. "She might be at the ruthenium mines. But I just found out that communication has been broken with the mine headquarters."

"Last week there were signs that someone was snooping around the mines," Till said. "Do you think there has been trouble?"

"I don't know," Arko said. "It could simply be interference from a meteor shower. I'll go to the mines and find out." He patted Till's shoulder. "Perhaps your mother is there, testing samples."

"Will you let us go with you?" Kleep asked.

"No," Arko said. "I want you to stay with Zibbit, where you will be safe. He is programmed to protect you."

He made a quick setting in Zibbit. "Now he is tuned in to the receiver on my landcraft," Arko said. "If you should need me, raise Zibbit's antenna. Remember . . . stay with Zibbit."

Zibbit clanked as he nodded. "Kleep will stay with Zibbit," he said. "I will protect her."

As soon as Arko left, Kleep said, "I don't think your mother is at the mines, or she would have told you she was going. I think she was kidnapped. That's why she only had time to leave part of a note."

"The only RU left would be the Ruzenians," Till said.

"Right," said Kleep. "It will be a long time before Grandfather comes back. I think we should go to Ruzena now and find out if Falda is there. The Ruzenians may have been snooping at the mine, trying to discover what the experiment is. They may have taken your mother and are planning to make her tell them about it."

"The work on the experiment hasn't been finished yet," Till said.

"The kidnappers wouldn't know that. Don't you want to go?" Kleep knew how worried Till must be. She knew if she had a chance to find her own mother, she wouldn't wait a minute.

Zibbit's head began to whirr. "You were told to stay with me." His voice came out in measured, metallic sounds.

"I'll be with you, Zibbit," Kleep said. "Wherever Till and I go, we'll take you, too. So you'll be with me. It's the same thing."

The whirring grew louder. "This does not sound right to me," Zibbit said.

Kleep sighed. "We need to find Till's mother. And we need you to come along and be brave, because we don't know what we'll discover. You *are* brave, aren't you?"

The tip of Zibbit's antenna wiggled. "I am programmed to be very brave," he said. "I will go with you."

"I'll get my landcraft!" Till said. He ran down the stairs.

"And I'll pack some food!" Kleep shouted after him.

In just a short time they were in the small land-craft. Zibbit and the basket of purple goppa fruit and meal-bread were tucked into the back seat.

Till pulled out a map and studied it. "As far as

I can tell, it will take us at least two hours at top speed to reach the edge of the Ruzena lands," he told Kleep.

"Then let's go!" Kleep said.

Till's guess was a good one. It was almost two hours later when they arrived at the edge of the bleak, rocky Desert of Stones. This desert divided the land explored by the colonists on Astarr from the land owned by the people of Ruzena.

Kleep was excited. She had never been this far from the colony before.

"The map shows an uncharted woods to the north of the Desert of Stones," Till told Kleep.

"I think I see it," Kleep said. She leaned forward in her seat. She felt something in her pocket bump against the panel in front of her.

"Oh-oh," Kleep said. "I still have Grandfather's superay glasses in my pocket."

Quickly they came close to the woods. The

trees ahead were very tall. They were so close together they were like a dark wall. Kleep looked at them and shivered.

Till pulled the control stick back sharply. The landcraft seemed to jump and shake.

"Something is pulling us down," he said.

Kleep put on the superay glasses. She looked out the window at the rocks below. "Those rocks are thick with some kind of ore," she said.

"It must be magnetite," Till said. "There must be lots of it to pull us down."

"I didn't know there was magnetite on this planet," Kleep said.

"Only the Ruzenians know," Till said. "They don't let us explore their land."

"Look!" Kleep suddenly shouted. "There's a small path down there. It seems to lead into the woods."

The path was narrow and almost covered with drooping branches. It looked frightening to

Kleep, but she wondered if it might lead the way to Ruzena.

Till brought the craft down to land near the path. As soon as the motor was turned off, Kleep threw open the door. She jumped out of the craft.

"Wait!" Zibbit whirred and sputtered. But Kleep did not wait. She ran to the path, where she stopped to look at the ground cover that had been beaten flat.

"Come with me!" Kleep shouted.

But suddenly she stopped, breathing hard.

There, blocking her way, was a huge, hairy creature with narrow black eyes and a large, cruel mouth.

He growled at Kleep, "Stay where you are! I'm Morgu, the Watchman of the Great Woods! No one can go past me into these woods! No one would dare try!"

CHAPTER

2

The Leather Braid Clue

Kleep took a deep breath. "But we're looking for someone!" Her voice came out in a squeak, and she tried again. "Morgu, we want to get to Ruzena to look for someone. Does this path go through the woods to Ruzena?"

Morgu's laugh was deep and rumbling. "Oh, yes!" he said. "The path goes to Ruzena, but *you* do not!"

Zibbit and Till had rushed to join Kleep. Zibbit, who was whirring and buzzing, hurried

to get between Kleep and the gigantic Morgu.

"You stay behind me," the robot said. "I will protect you."

Kleep peered out from behind Zibbit. "Why not?" she asked Morgu. "Why can't we go down this path?"

His little eyes flashed. He bent so low that she could feel his stale breath on her face. A braided leather tie that he wore around his neck dangled in front of her nose. "Because I say so. I am the

Watchman paid by King Rurik of Ruzena to keep people from entering the Great Woods."

Kleep stopped being afraid of Morgu. She became angry instead. "Then we'll just find another way!" she said.

Morgu stretched tall and scratched his chest. "There is no other path. Besides, there are dangers in the forest that would keep you from Ruzena!"

"What dangers?" Till asked.

"You'll never find out!" Morgu said. "You must go away."

"I do not like this," Zibbit said. "We should go back to the landcraft and contact Arko."

Morgu stepped closer to them. His little eyes were greedy. "Don't go yet," he said. "Give me something and I will answer your questions."

Before Kleep could say anything, Till pulled at her arm. "All right," he said to Morgu. "Wait here while we talk about it."

Till pulled Kleep back to the landcraft. Zibbit was close behind them.

"Kleep!" Till whispered. "Did you see that leather braid Morgu is wearing?"

"Yes," Kleep said.

"I think it's my mother's belt. It looks just like one she made only last week. What if Morgu has done something to my mother?"

Kleep gripped his arm. "Morgu hasn't hurt your mother, Till. Someone else had to be with your mother. I think this proves they came this way. Morgu probably let them enter the woods, because they were from Ruzena."

"Let's ask him," Till said.

"We'd better take him something, if we want him to answer us," Kleep said. She picked up the basket of food.

When they came near Morgu, Kleep put some of the purple goppa fruit on a rock. "You can have that," she said, "if you answer our questions."

Morgu stuffed the fruit into his mouth and chewed greedily.

"Where did you get that leather braid you're wearing?" Kleep asked.

"It's pretty. I wanted it," he said.

"Did a woman give it to you?"

"Give me more food."

"Answer the question first and I will."

"It was a woman," Morgu said. He reached

out and snatched the basket from Kleep. He stuffed the rest of the food into his mouth and threw down the basket.

"Was the woman with people from Ruzena?" Kleep asked.

"Give me something else," Morgu said.

"We don't have anything else," Kleep said.

Without any warning Morgu jumped toward Kleep. He grabbed the superay glasses that were sticking out of the top of her pocket.

"Don't touch those!" Kleep shouted. "They belong to my grandfather. And they are special glasses. When you look through them . . ."

But it was too late. Morgu had put them on his nose. He looked down at Kleep, Till, and Zibbit. He let out a loud roar.

"He sees our bones!" Kleep whispered to Till. "Let's scare him!"

So Kleep and Till began to shout and wave their arms at Morgu.

"I am programmed to be brave!" Zibbit said. He marched toward Morgu and beat at his large, hairy legs.

Morgu was frightened. "Bones! I only see bones!" he shouted. In his fear he grabbed Zibbit. With one hand he threw Zibbit against a tree. With the other hand Morgu pulled off the glasses and threw them to the ground. He ran off through the woods and disappeared behind some large rocks.

Quickly Kleep picked up the glasses and stuffed them back into her pocket.

"Kleep!" Till shouted. "Zibbit's left arm! Morgu pulled it off!"

"Oh, poor Zibbit!" Kleep gasped.

Zibbit was back on his feet, waving his left arm in his right hand as though it were a weapon. "I will fight to protect you, Kleep!" His words whirred and clanged.

Kleep looked around. Morgu was still out of

sight. "This is our chance!" she said. "Run! Into the woods before Morgu comes back!"

Till led the way. Kleep took Zibbit's right arm, and they ran down the dark and twisting path into the woods.

Finally, Till and Kleep were out of breath. They stopped and leaned against some trees.

"I have to rest a minute," Kleep panted.

"Not for long," Till said. "When Morgu gets over being afraid, he will come after us. We had better go as far as we can into the woods and try to find Ruzena."

"Maybe we can reach Arko and tell him where we are," Kleep said. She raised Zibbit's antenna, but nothing happened.

"I think the circuit's broken," Till said. "Maybe Zibbit can attach his arm again."

"I cannot repair myself," Zibbit said.

Kleep looked at the mass of wires inside Zibbit's arm. She didn't know where to begin. "I can *try* to put Zibbit's arm back," she said. "But I really don't know how."

Till looked back down the path. "I don't think we should spend any more time here," he said. "Morgu could come after us."

Kleep looked back too. She couldn't see Morgu. She couldn't hear him. Everything was deathly quiet. She had the feeling that something terrible was going to happen!

CHAPTER
3
Attack of the Giant Worms

The forest soon became so dark they couldn't see the path. Suddenly Till stopped, and Kleep and Zibbit bumped into him.

"We've got to find a place to spend the night," Till said.

"We should hide away from this path," Kleep said, "in case Morgu comes along. I'm surprised he hasn't come back by now."

"Maybe he's waiting until morning to follow us," Till said.

"Morgu talked about dangers in these woods,"

Kleep said. She looked around nervously. "He must know something about the Great Woods that we don't know."

Till looked up. "It might be a good idea for us to climb a tree. That way we will be out of sight and we can keep a watch for Morgu."

"What if we go to sleep and fall out of the tree?" Kleep asked.

"Zibbit will hang on to us with his good arm," Till said. "Robots don't sleep."

"Robots do not climb trees, either," Zibbit said.

"That's no problem," Kleep said. "We can pull Zibbit up into the tree. He's not that heavy."

"I'll boost you up," Till said to Kleep. "See if you can reach a branch."

Kleep reached high. She caught a strong branch and began to pull herself upward. Soon she was wedged into a spot against the trunk of the tree.

"Till, there is something wrong with these trees," Kleep said. "The bark is gone from the lower part. Some of the lower branches are gone, too. And the bushes!" Kleep went on. "I know why they seemed strange to me before. Something has stripped them of their leaves."

Till just shrugged. "I'll lift Zibbit up to you," he said. "Are you ready? We don't have much time. It's getting darker every second."

"Go ahead," Kleep told him.

She reached down and tugged Zibbit, as Till pushed, until Zibbit was securely up in the perch she had found. Then she and Zibbit helped Till up.

"I wish you hadn't given Morgu all the food," Till said. "I'm hungry."

"We had to give it to him," Kleep reminded Till. "It wasn't my fault!"

"I didn't say it was your fault!"

"Well, you said . . ." Kleep stopped. "We're

both hungry and tired. And we're worried about your mother."

"I'm sorry I was rude," Till said.

"I know how you feel," Kleep told him. She remembered that two years ago her mother and father had left for a space mission to Earth. They had never come back. Kleep planned to study to be a spacecraft pilot. She wanted to go to Earth to find her parents.

The moon rose. Kleep was glad she could now see what was around them.

"I'm going to try to put your arm back where it should be," she said to Zibbit. "Then maybe I can reach Grandfather."

She peered into Zibbit's tangle of wires. There were so many loose ends. She attached them to the other loose wire ends. "How am I doing, Zibbit?" she asked.

"Glibble. Glibble globble," Zibbit said. He began to buzz. His ears lit up.

"Oh, no!" Kleep said. "I think I'm making things worse." She quickly unfastened the wires.

"That felt very strange," Zibbit said.

Till pulled Zibbit's antenna as high as it would go. "Maybe this will help," he said.

Kleep studied the wires as well as she could in the dim, greenish light. She fastened two wires together. "Now," she said, "let's see what happens."

There was a crackling sound, and a voice said, "Come in. Come in, Kleep. Is that you?"

"Grandfather!" Kleep said. "We're up in a tree! We're in the Great Woods of Ruzena!"

"Oh, no!" Till suddenly shouted. He grabbed Kleep's arm.

She turned so quickly that the wires fell apart. "Now look what you've done!" she cried. "I'll never remember which two I had fastened together! And I don't think Grandfather heard me!"

33

"Never mind that," Till said. "Just look at what's happening below us!"

Kleep stared down at the ground. It seemed to be moving. She heard a strange snapping, crunching sound. As her eyes grew used to the dark movement, she saw a mass of giant worms crawling from holes in the ground. They were eating the shrubbery and the bark of the trees. They were eating everything in sight!

Kleep was afraid to move. Now she knew why Morgu hadn't come after them! What if the worms discovered them up here in the tree? What would they do?

It didn't take long to find out. Hunching, sliding, some of the worms crawled over each other trying to get to the tree in which Kleep, Till, and Zibbit were sitting.

Some of them stretched up the sides of the tree. Kleep screamed and pulled up her feet. She saw the worms stretch up, then slide back.

34

"They're coming up after us!" she gasped.

"I don't think they can make it up the smooth trunk where the bark is gone," Till said. "They seem to be slipping back."

But Kleep watched one of the largest and fattest of the worms. It wiggled over the bodies of the other worms as though they were stair steps. It came closer and closer, up the side of the tree. Its mouth was open, showing rows of tiny, pointed teeth. Its little round eyes seemed to be staring right at Kleep!

CHAPTER

4

The Wall of Music

"Till!" Kleep said. "Hold tightly to Zibbit. I'll hold Zibbit too! Whatever you do, don't let go!"

She leaned down from the branch and hit the worm over its slimy head with Zibbit's left arm. "Ugh!" she said, as the worm fell back into the crawling mass of worms under the tree.

"Good work!" Till said.

"Do you think we should try to climb higher?" Kleep asked him.

"I don't think we should take the chance," Till said. "Remember, Zibbit is too clumsy to climb trees."

Zibbit whirred and stared at Till. "But Zibbit is good at hitting worms on the head," he said.

"Don't feel unhappy, Zibbit," Kleep told him. "I don't know what we'd do without you and your arm."

"I have a strong arm," Zibbit said. He didn't look at Till.

Kleep and Till took turns watching the worms during the night. Most of them didn't venture up into the tree. Those who did found themselves knocked to the ground again by Zibbit's arm.

Finally the worms began sliding back into their holes. Kleep looked up to see daylight touching the sky. She gave a long sigh of relief.

"I think we're safe from the worms until it gets dark again," she said.

"But we're not sure we're safe from Morgu," Till said. "I think we'd better get started right away."

It was easier to get out of the tree than it was

to climb into it. When they were all on the ground, Kleep shook her head. Till looked tired, and his clothes were torn. Zibbit's once-shiny body was dull and scratched. Kleep put a hand to her hair and felt a mass of tangles.

"I hope we aren't far from Ruzena," she said. "I'm worried about your mother."

Till grabbed her arm. "Be quiet," he said. "Listen!"

As Kleep stood still she could hear something behind them in the distance. It was crashing and roaring. The sounds were coming closer.

"Morgu!" she said. "He's after us!"

"I will fight him!" Zibbit said.

"No!" Till said. "Let's get as far away from him as we can! Run!"

They raced down the path. Kleep, gasping for breath, cried, "Look! There's a patch of light!"

"The end of the Great Woods!" Till called. "Ruzena!"

Morgu was coming closer. Kleep raced to stay ahead of his crashing feet.

Suddenly everything seemed to turn into a slow-motion dream. Kleep was running, but she was staying in the same place. She was hurrying, but her feet were barely moving. A song beat against her ears like a wall of music. The rhythm of the music pushed her back. She couldn't understand the words that tried to fill her brain. She could see Till ahead of her, holding his hands against his ears. Only Zibbit was not touched by the music.

"The trees are singing!" Zibbit said.

"Don't give up! We can sing too!" Kleep shouted.

"What?" Till asked.

"Sing something. Anything. Sing as loudly as you can! You too, Zibbit!" Kleep yelled.

At the top of her lungs, Kleep sang a marching song. At first she could barely hear Till, who was

singing an old folk tune. Zibbit was not programmed to sing. But he whirred and buzzed
and beat an uneven, clanging rhythm on his
metal chest.

Kleep wanted to laugh, because they sounded
so awful. But she pushed ahead. She found it
wasn't as hard to move against the wall of music.
They were breaking the rhythm of the trees.

The music of the trees grew weaker. Then it
stopped. The wall of music was gone.

"We're almost there!" Kleep cried. "Keep
singing and run!"

Her voice was drowned out by a roar coming
from behind her. "Hurry!" she screamed.
"Morgu!"

With her last bit of energy she staggered from
the woods into a clearing. As she tried to catch
her breath, Kleep looked up to see a large building with a spacecraft moored beside it. Smaller
buildings were around it. And here and there in

the clearing were small, white-haired, bow-legged people who were staring at Kleep, Till, and Zibbit. They looked angry.

Then Morgu rushed from behind her into the clearing.

The small people jumped up and down in

anger. They hurried toward the intruders, shouting and waving their fists. Some of them picked up clubs and stones. A group of soldiers appeared.

"We're trapped!" Kleep said. "What will we do?"

CHAPTER
5
A Plan of Escape

The small people rushed at Morgu, driving him back into the woods.

"You are to keep people from coming through the Great Woods!" they shouted at him. "How did these people get here?"

"They tricked me!" Morgu grumbled. He turned and ran back down the path, crashing his way through the woods, roaring and complaining.

The small people were threatening as they surrounded Till, Kleep, and Zibbit. Several soldiers grabbed them and pushed them past the spacecraft, through a courtyard, and into the big building.

Kleep, Till, and Zibbit were marched down a stairway made of rough stone, into a damp underground prison.

"Let us talk to someone!" Kleep said to the soldiers. But no one answered her.

They came to a large cell. One of the men took out a key and opened a heavy wooden door. Before Kleep could say another word, she was pushed into the room. Till and Zibbit followed. The door was shut behind them. Kleep heard the key turn in the lock. The only light in the room came from a torch on the wall. The torch was made from a twist of the slow-burning gar plant. Its sap oozed in a steady flame.

"Till! Kleep!" It was Falda!

She hugged the children. She shook Zibbit's good hand.

"I had hoped you would understand my message. It was all I had time to write. Where is Arko?" Suddenly she stopped talking and stared at them. "Where is Arko?" she asked again. "You didn't come alone, did you?"

"We were in a hurry to find you, Mother," Till said. "No one was sure what had happened to you. Arko went to look for you at the ruthenium mines."

"How did you get here?" Kleep asked.

"Some of the Ruzenians kidnapped me," Falda said. "Their King Rurik thinks we are making a secret war weapon with the ruthenium, because it is used in rockets, too. He thinks we are planning to attack his kingdom. He insists that I give him the plans."

"Didn't you tell him that you are working on an outer-space anchor for spacecraft?" Till asked.

"Yes," Falda said. "But he didn't believe me. I

tried to explain that our project isn't finished. We are hoping to find something that will combine with the ruthenium to hold tightly to the small spacecraft."

"Oh," Kleep said softly. "I wonder if magnetite would work?"

Falda didn't hear Kleep. She sighed. "The king only became angry. He shouted that tomorrow morning I must give him the war weapon plans."

Till put an arm around her shoulders. "Don't worry, Mother," he said. "We'll think of some way to make the king believe the truth."

"If he won't believe your mother, he won't believe us, either," Kleep said. "I think we should try to escape."

"I am programmed to protect you," Zibbit said.

"That's not all you're programmed for!" Till said. He shoved Zibbit's left arm into Falda's hands. "If you can repair Zibbit, Mother, we can contact Arko and get help! Zibbit is tuned in to the receiver on Arko's landcraft!"

Falda was so excited that her hands shook. "Of course I can repair Zibbit! Someone, please! Hold the torch so I can get more light!"

Kleep pulled the twist of burning gar plant from the wall and held it close to Zibbit. She tried to stay calm, but it was hard for her to breathe.

At last Falda straightened, gave a pat to Zibbit's shoulder, and said, "He's as good as new."

Till peered through the small window in the door. "No one is in the hallway," he said. "Let's try to reach Arko."

Falda raised Zibbit's antenna to its full length and said, "Come in, Arko. This is Falda. I have Kleep and Till with me."

They waited, but there was no answer. "Come

in, Arko," Falda said again. Finally she shook her head. "We're below ground level, and the walls of this building are thick. Our signal can't get through."

"Some good has come of this," Zibbit said. "My arm is in its right place."

"So much for escaping," Till grumbled.

But Kleep went to the door. She bent and rubbed her fingers over the lock. Then she looked at the torch she was holding. "This should give us just the heat and light we'll need," she said.

"For what?" Falda asked.

Kleep took the superay glasses from her pocket. "These are powerful," she said. "I think they'll magnify the heat enough so the lock on the door will melt. It seems to be made of some weak metal."

Falda hurried to the door and bent to study the lock. "You're right," she said. "It's a poor alloy, and it's old. I think we can do it, but it will take time."

"We can start now!" Till said.

"No," Falda told them. "Not until after they bring our evening meal. There might be soldiers coming to check on us before then. After we eat they'll probably leave us alone."

"Maybe we could just soften it a bit," Kleep said, but Falda shook her head. Kleep put the gar plant back in its holder. She hoped the king wouldn't become impatient and send for Falda before morning.

Finally, two soldiers entered with plates of fruit and a red cheese that tasted sweet. Kleep gulped down her food and handed the plate back to a soldier.

One of the soldiers studied Zibbit. "Maybe the king will let us have the robot for our own," he said to the other soldier. "We could take him now. We could see what he can do."

He pulled Zibbit toward him. Zibbit made whirring, clanking noises and fell over in a heap.

"Go ahead," Till said. "Take him. He's not a good robot. He breaks down. He gets orders mixed up. And he's ugly."

The soldier poked Zibbit with his boot. He mumbled something under his breath, then grabbed the plates from Falda and Till. The two soldiers stomped from the cell and slammed the heavy door.

No one moved until they could no longer hear the soldiers' footsteps. Then Zibbit managed to stand.

"I am *not* ugly," he said to Till. "It was good that you helped me make them think I could not work well. But you did not have to say I was ugly."

"Of course you're not ugly," Till said. "I only told them that because I was afraid they would take you away."

"You're the best-looking robot on Astarr," Kleep said to Zibbit. She quickly pulled the gar plant from the wall. "Here, Zibbit. You hold the superay glasses in front of the lock."

"Let's hope this works," Till said.

Kleep nodded. "And let's hope we don't get caught!"

CHAPTER
6
A Fateful Meeting

For a long time they worked, stopping only once when they heard footsteps in the hallway. No one moved until the sound faded away.

Finally Kleep whispered, "It's melting! The lock is coming apart!"

"Good!" Till said. "I think it's nearly morning."

Kleep tugged at the door, and the lock gave way. The door flew open. "Let's go!" she whispered. "No one is in sight! Come on!"

Quietly they went into the hallway. Falda

whispered, "If we can get to the king's spacecraft, do you think you can pilot it, Till?"

"Yes," Till said. "Don't anyone make a sound. We must be very quiet." He glared at Zibbit, who tried to walk carefully but clanked at every step.

"Do not blame me for the noise," Zibbit said. "A robot who spends the night in a tree needs oiling."

They crept up the stairs and through the main hall. Till slowly opened the door to the courtyard and looked through. "It's early," he said. "Everyone must be asleep. I don't see any soldiers."

"Hurry!" Falda said. "Let's get in the craft!"

Kleep led the way, eased open the large door to the craft, and climbed in.

"We'd better get Zibbit inside," she said. "You push and I'll pull."

"Ready..." Till began. But in her hurry

Kleep pulled too soon, and Zibbit swung against the side of the craft with a loud clang.

"Be careful!" Till gave an extra push, and Zibbit tumbled into the spacecraft.

Till reached out a hand to his mother, but his arm was struck by a soldier who seemed to have come from nowhere. Other soldiers ran toward them from the far side of the spacecraft.

Falda and Till struggled with the soldiers.

"I will help!" Zibbit whirred. He moved toward the open door.

"Wait!" Kleep shouted. She quickly raised Zibbit's antenna and cried, "Grandfather! Arko! Come in! This is Kleep, and we need help!"

There was a crackle, and Kleep said, "We're in the courtyard of the King of Ruzena! He has taken us prisoners! Grandfather, if you can hear me . . ."

But strong arms closed around her, and she and Zibbit were pulled from the craft.

"Did you get through?" Falda whispered to Kleep.

"I don't know," Kleep said. The soldiers were small, but they were very angry. She didn't know what they would do.

There was a commotion at the door to the building, and a short, wide person wearing a tall, shiny crown, a wrinkled sleeping robe, and an angry frown stomped through the door and over to the spacecraft.

"Who is disturbing my sleep?" he growled. He stared at each of them. "So! It's our prisoners!" he added. "Were they trying to escape? Well, back to the cell with them!"

Kleep knew that if Arko got her message he would call the gardas, the Astarr protectors. Their speedcrafts were fast. But Kleep knew she would have to stall for time.

She slowly pulled the superay glasses from her pocket and put them on. She leaned forward and stared at the king.

He did just what she hoped he would do. "What are you doing?" he cried. "Is that another weapon? Take those things off her face!"

One of the soldiers pulled them from Kleep.

"My grandfather is an inventor. Falda is his assistant," Kleep said to the king. "Those glasses are one of his inventions. Why don't you try them?"

The king looked suspicious, but he reached for the glasses and put them on. He gasped. "You have all turned into bones!"

"Will you please listen?" Kleep asked him. "Falda can tell you about the ruthenium."

"We aren't working on a weapon," Falda began, as the king stared through the glasses at everyone around him.

She went on to explain about their project. The king interrupted her only once. He pointed at Zibbit and said, "He needs oiling."

When Falda had finished, the king took off the glasses, glared at her, and said, "We will talk about this tomorrow. You will go back to your cell and . . ."

His words were drowned out by the loud hiss of a speedcraft as it circled the courtyard and

settled just behind King Rurik. The door opened, and out jumped six large gardas and Arko.

King Rurik backed away so fast that he bumped into his soldiers.

"Oh, Grandfather! Am I glad to see you!" Kleep shouted.

Arko nodded at Kleep. He looked very serious, but Kleep could tell that he was glad to see her, too.

"This is King Rurik," Falda said to Arko. "He

thought you and I were working on a weapon that would be dangerous to his people. But I've explained about the docking system we are trying to perfect."

Arko stepped forward and said to the king, "I would like to tell you more about our project. I hope you'll visit our mines and see what we are trying to do."

"Visit your mines?" King Rurik's eyes glittered, and Kleep wondered what he was thinking. She didn't trust him.

The king looked up at Arko and the large gardas. He waved to his own soldiers to step away from their prisoners. "I might visit your mines," he said, "even if these unfriendly people *did* invade my lands."

Kleep opened her mouth to say that wasn't true, but Arko signaled her to keep quiet.

The king lifted the superay glasses and stared at Arko through them. "If you mean what you say and come on peaceful terms, then I think you should prove it by letting me keep these."

"It will be my pleasure," Arko said politely.

"Don't be upset," Falda whispered to Kleep. "Arko can easily make another pair."

"Then all of you may go," King Rurik said.

Without a word Kleep and Till took Zibbit's arms and helped him into the speedcraft. They climbed into the back and leaned against the cushions. Kleep sighed. She was very tired.

"I want to show Arko and Falda that field of magnetite," she said. "If that magnetite would work with the ruthenium, maybe the Ruzenians and our people could work together in peace, sharing the project."

"I don't trust that king," Till said.

Kleep sighed. "Neither do I."

"We were very brave," Zibbit said proudly.

Kleep smiled at Till and Zibbit. "We make a good team," she said.

The gardas helped Falda and Till into the speedcraft, and it took off with a rush of air.

Kleep looked down at the small king, who was clinging to his sleeping robe and his crown. She shivered.

"What's the matter?" Till asked.

"I have a strong feeling," Kleep said, "that we're going to have other adventures to-gether . . . and very soon."